TIG HUNT

Judy Waite
Illustrated by Holly Swain

RIGBY

Chapter 1

Becky was staring out of the window.

"What are you doing?" said Miss Ross angrily.

"I saw something strange over by the wood," said Becky.

Miss Ross looked at Becky. "What sort
of something?" she said.

"I think it was a tiger," said Becky.

Everyone ran to the window.

"Sit down at once," said Miss Ross. She was still angry. "There isn't a tiger in the wood," she said. "We don't have tigers in this country."

Becky grinned at me. "I was only joking," she whispered.

But I didn't grin back . . .

. . . because I really **did** see something!

Just then, Cathy Moon burst into the classroom.

"Late again, Cathy," said Miss Ross sternly. "That's the third time this week."

7

"Would you come and look for the
tiger with me at play-time?" I whispered
to Becky.

"There isn't a tiger," said Becky.
"I was only joking."

"Please," I said.

"All right then, just this once,"
said Becky.

Where do tigers live?

At play-time, Becky and I went over to the wood together. We waited and waited, but we didn't hear any tigers.

"Let's go," said Becky, "there's no tiger here."

Suddenly I saw something. "Look!"
I said. "Over there!"

There was something orange and
fluffy hanging on a bush.
"It's tiger fur!" whispered Becky.
"There is a tiger after all!"

Just then, the bell rang.

"We have to go back now," said Becky.

"Let's come back at lunchtime," I said.

At lunchtime we sat beside Matt Clark because he knows all about tigers.

"Do tigers eat people?" I asked.

"They like to eat people best of all," said Matt.

Suddenly, I didn't want to go into the wood again.

Chapter 2

Matt, Becky and I went back to the wood.
We kept close together. Suddenly,
Matt stopped.

"What was that?" he whispered.

tigers
are
great

Then we saw it! It was orange and had stripes. It was creeping through the bushes. All three of us screamed! We turned and ran . . .

. . . straight into Miss Ross!

"What are you doing?" said Miss
Ross sternly.

"We saw the tiger," I gasped.

"It's in the wood," said Becky.

"We're lucky to be alive," said Matt,
"because tigers can pounce from twenty
metres. They bound forwards suddenly,
baring their claws. Then they bite
your neck!"

"That will do!" said Miss Ross.
"I've told you all before, there is no
tiger in the wood." She marched off
into the wood.

"Goodbye, Miss Ross," we whispered.
We closed our eyes and waited for
the scream.

But we didn't hear a scream. We heard
Miss Ross demand, "COME OUT AT ONCE!"

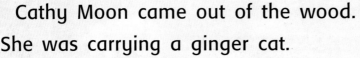

Cathy Moon came out of the wood.
She was carrying a ginger cat.

"I was feeding my cat, Miss Ross,"
said Cathy. "I feed her in the morning
before school and at lunchtime. I keep
her in the wood because my mum says
I can't take her home."

Miss Ross looked at Cathy for a
long time.

"The cat could live at my house,"
said Miss Ross. "You live near me,
don't you, Cathy? You could come and
visit her."

Miss Ross didn't sound angry any more.

"What's your cat called?" I asked.
"Tiger," said Cathy.
"So, there was a Tiger in the wood after all," grinned Becky.

Miss Ross stroked Tiger's striped ears.
Tiger purred and purred.
"Poor little Tiger," whispered Miss Ross.
She didn't sound angry at all.

Miss Ross took Tiger from Cathy. She put one arm around Cathy's shoulder.

"Come on," she said, "let's take Tiger into school."

Becky, Matt and I followed them.

Suddenly, Becky shouted, "There's something strange in the sky!"

We all looked up.

"Only joking!" she laughed.

I didn't laugh back . . .

. . . because I really **did** see something!